TMNT

TURTLES TOGETHER

By Benjamin Harper
Illustrated by Artful Doodlers

simon
scribbles

New York   London   Toronto   Sydney

Based on the film TMNT™ by Imagi Animation Studios and Warner Bros.

An imprint of Simon & Schuster Children's Publishing Division
1230 Avenue of the Americas, New York, NY 10020
© 2007 Mirage Studios, Inc. *Teenage Mutant Ninja Turtles*™ and TMNT
are trademarks of Mirage Studios, Inc. All rights reserved.

SIMON SCRIBBLES and associated colophon are trademarks of Simon & Schuster, Inc.
All rights reserved, including the right of reproduction in whole or in part in any form.
Manufactured in the United States of America
First Edition
2 4 6 8 10 9 7 5 3 1
ISBN-13: 978-1-4169-3412-7
ISBN-10: 1-4169-3412-X

The Teenage Mutant Ninja Turtles are back!

Leonardo's favorite weapons are katana!

Leonardo is training in Central America
to become the group's leader.

A village is under attack!

Through the Jungle!

Follow the maze to help Leonardo get through the jungle and save the village!

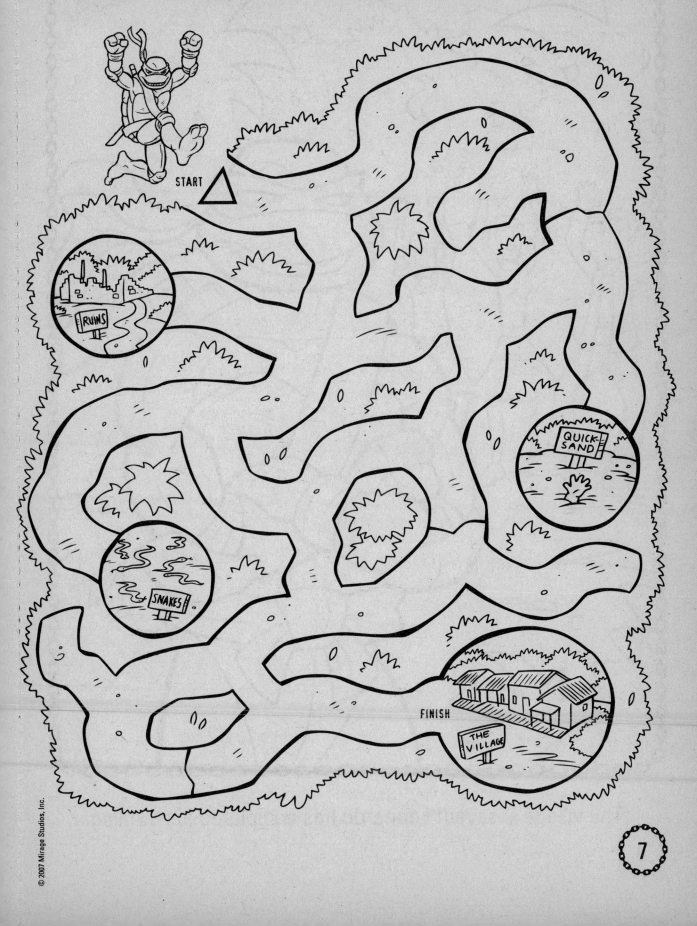

The village is saved! Leonardo has completed his training.

Raphael uses sais in battle.

The Nightwatcher fights crime in New York City.

10

Caught in the act!

The Nightwatcher has ended another criminal's career!

Guess Who!

Who is the Nightwatcher?
Write the first letter of each object on the lines below to find out.

$$\underline{} \ \underline{} \ \underline{} \ \underline{} \ \underline{} \ \underline{} \ \underline{}$$

1 2 3 4 5 6 7

Another busy night of fighting crime is over.

Michelangelo uses nunchakus!

"Take that, turtle nerd!" the kids scream.

Party Time

Cowabunga Carl's busy at the birthday party.
Circle the things you might find there!

Cowabunga Carl grabs some birthday
cake on his way out.

Cowabunga, Dudes!

Find out who Cowabunga Carl is by writing the letter from the alphabet that comes before each letter below.

N J D I F M B O H F M P

– – – – – – – – – – – – –

Michelangelo's home! Down into the sewers he goes!

Whoosh! Michelangelo's off through
the sewers on his skateboard.

21

Skateboarding in the Sewers

When you're a ninja, everything's a test!

Follow the maze to help Michelangelo find his way home.

Donatello has mastered the bo staff.

Donatello likes to work on gadgets.

24

Donatello can see what's happening all over the city!

Sensei Surprise

Splinter is the Turtles' teacher.

Connect the dots to see what he looks like.

The Turtles' lair!

Hide-and-Seek

Find and circle the four Turtles.

April O'Neil and Casey Jones are the Turtles' friends.

April brings back an important artifact in a sealed box.

Casey Quiz

What is Casey's favorite sport?
See if you can guess from the clues on this page.

WRITE YOUR ANSWER HERE: _____.

Techno Time

If you create your own special device to help the Turtles, they'll put it to good use! *Draw a picture of your device, and then write what it does.*

Leonardo's on his way home.

He jumps!

The brothers are together again!

Nobody panic! Donatello just messed up an experiment.

April and Casey deliver the artifact to Mr. Winters.

Match the Statues

Find and circle the two statues that look exactly the same.

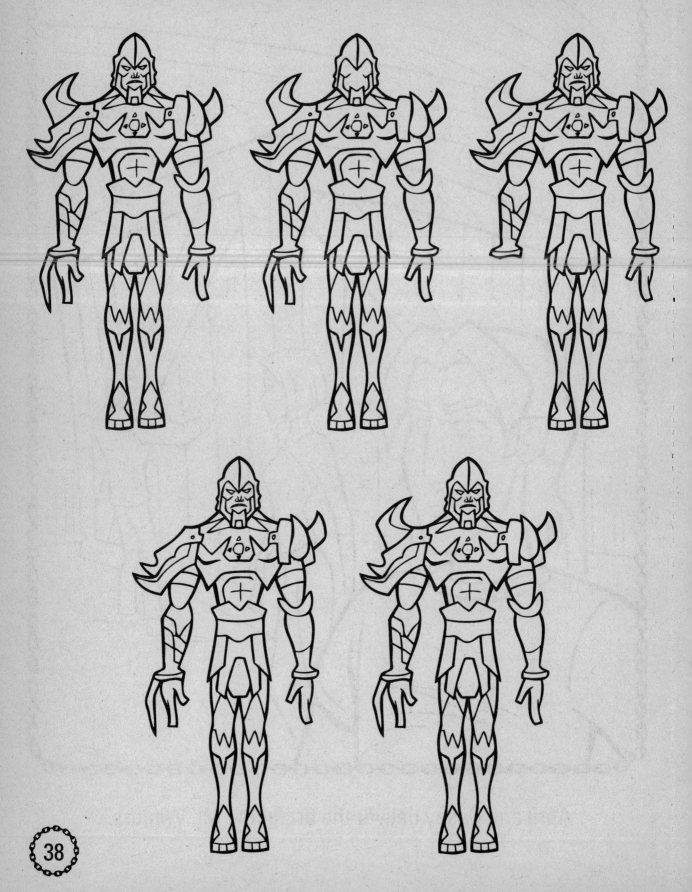

The Legend of Yaotl!

Yaotl and his four Generals prepare for battle!

Aguila is the Generals' leader.

When the Stars of Kikin line up, a portal opens!

Monsters attack!

Monster Time

Draw your own portal monster.

The Foot Clan of ninjas works for Winters!

Spot the Ninjas

Ninjas are good at hiding.

Find and circle the twelve ninjas in this picture.

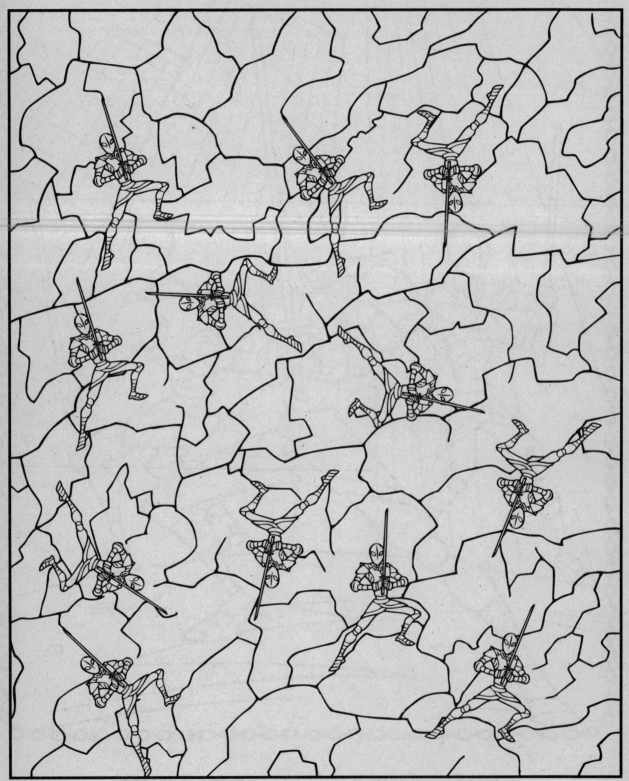

Karai is the leader of the Foot Clan.

Turtle training!

The Turtles run into the Foot Clan.

Battle Surprise

What else do the Turtles run into?
Connect the dots to find out!

Raphael and the monster duke it out!

The Generals arrive and capture the monster.

General Match

Draw lines from the Generals to their matching animals.

GENERAL AGUILA

GENERAL MONO

GENERAL SERPIENTE

GENERAL GATO

The Generals bring the creature to Winters.

Cowabunga Crossword

Try out your turtle power on this crossword.
Fill your answers into the boxes below.

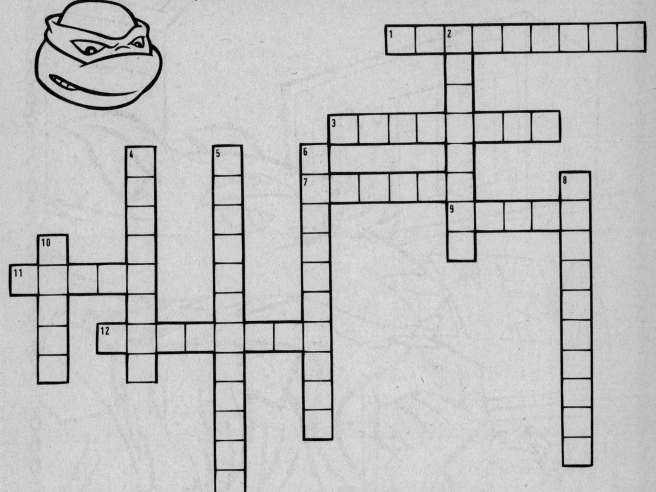

ACROSS:

1. THIS TURTLE LOVES TO WORK WITH ELECTRONICS
3. THE TURTLES' ARCHENEMIES
7. HE'S THE LEADER OF THE FOUR GENERALS
9. THE LEADER OF THE FOOT CLAN
11. THESE STARS LINE UP TO OPEN THE PORTAL
12. THE TURTLES' LEADER

DOWN:

2. MICHELANGELO'S FAVORITE WEAPON
4. THE TURTLES' TEACHER
5. HE FIGHTS CRIME ON A MOTORCYCLE
6. HE LOVES TO PLAY HOCKEY
8. IN HIS SPARE TIME, MICHELANGELO LIKES TO PLAY THESE
10. THE TEENAGE MUTANT NINJA TURTLES' FAVORITE FOOD

Splinter wants to know who's controlling the monsters.

The Nightwatcher takes to the streets.

Monster Match

The Generals capture more monsters. *Draw lines to match the top part of each monster with its matching bottom part.*

Casey tries to fight the Nightwatcher!

Busted!

Who discovers the Nightwatcher's secret identity? *To find out, write the letter that matches each number on the lines below.*

| 14 | 12 | 80 | 1 | 39 | | 72 | 5 | 22 | 1 | 80 |

CODE:

A=12	G=99	M=10	S=80	Y=39
B=2	H=3	N=22	T=46	Z=18
C=14	I=15	O=5	U=100	
D=11	J=72	P=33	V=4	
E=1	K=7	Q=40	W=9	
F=6	L=0	R=55	X=8	

Hockey Time

You can wear Casey Jones's hockey mask. *With an adult's help,*
cut out the mask along the dashed lines. Poke a hole on either
side of the mask, then tie a string through the holes,
so that it fits around your head.

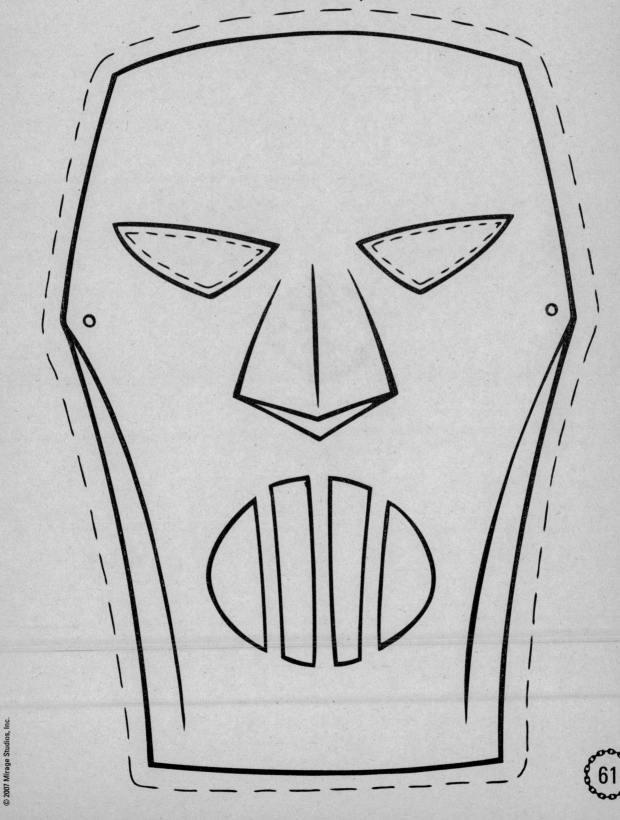

Another monster attacks!

The Generals catch it — and the Foot Clan helps!

Kitty Caper

General Gato is chasing Casey and Raphael!
Follow the maze to help them escape.

START

FINISH

April tells the Turtles all about Yaotl!

Raphael flips out!

Wicked Word Search

Cowabunga! *Find the words from the list below and circle them in any direction.*

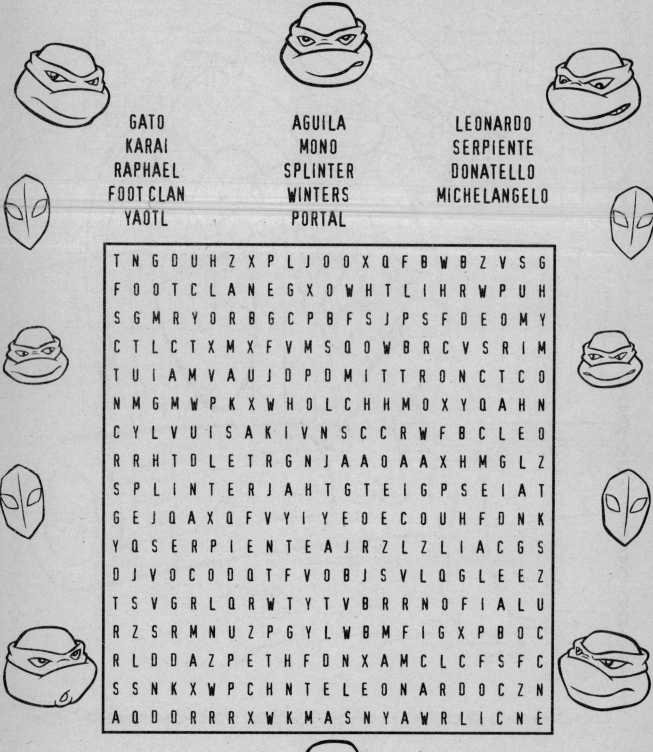

GATO
KARAI
RAPHAEL
FOOT CLAN
YAOTL

AGUILA
MONO
SPLINTER
WINTERS
PORTAL

LEONARDO
SERPIENTE
DONATELLO
MICHELANGELO

```
T N G D U H Z X P L J O O X Q F B W B Z V S G
F O O T C L A N E G X O W H T L I H R W P U H
S G M R Y O R B G C P B F S J P S F D E O M Y
C T L C T X M X F V M S Q O W B R C V S R I M
T U I A M V A U J D P D M I T T R O N C T C O
N M G M W P K X W H O L C H H M O X Y Q A H N
C Y L V U I S A K I V N S C C R W F B C L E O
R R H T D L E T R G N J A A O A A X H M G L Z
S P L I N T E R J A H T G T E I G P S E I A T
G E J Q A X Q F V Y I Y E O E C O U H F D N K
Y Q S E R P I E N T E A J R Z L Z L I A C G S
D J V O C O D Q T F V O B J S V L Q G L E E Z
T S V G R L Q R W T Y T V B R R N O F I A L U
R Z S R M N U Z P G Y L W B M F I G X P B O C
R L D D A Z P E T H F D N X A M C L C F S F C
S S N K X W P C H N T E L E O N A R D O C Z N
A Q D D R R R X W K M A S N Y A W R L I C N E
```

Kikin Code

The Stars of Kikin are aligned! *Find out where the portal will open again by writing the letter in the alphabet that comes before each letter below.*

O F X   Z P S L   D J U Z !

_ _ _   _ _ _ _   _ _ _ _ !

Michelangelo keeps busy playing video games.

The Nightwatcher fights a monster!

Monster Twins

Find and circle the two monsters that look exactly the same.

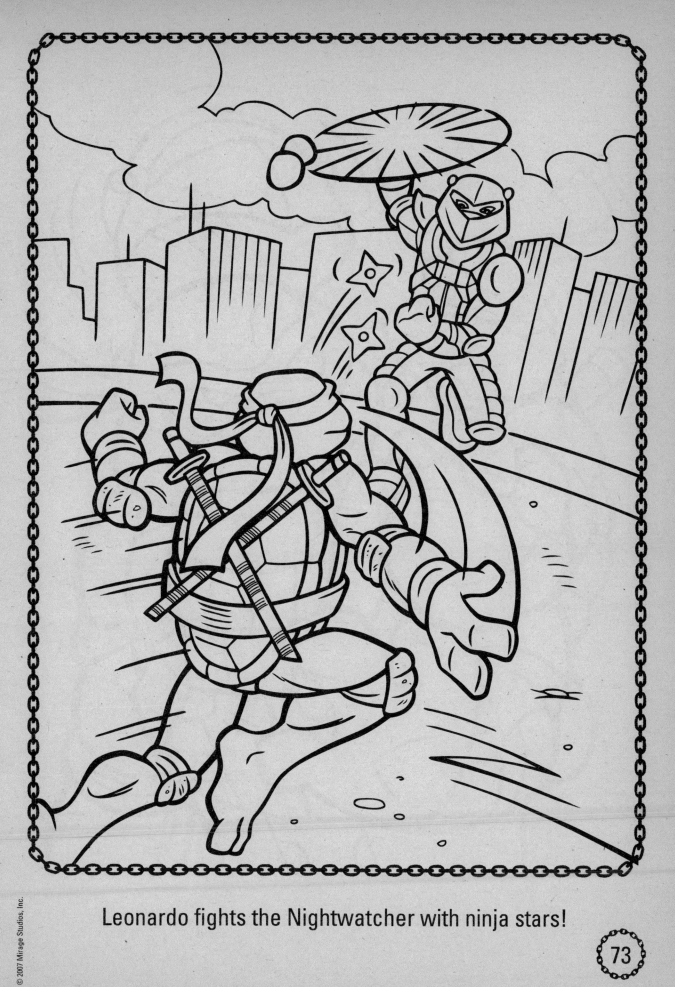

Leonardo fights the Nightwatcher with ninja stars!

The Nightwatcher's true identity is revealed.

Oh, no! The Generals captured Leonardo.

Legends Live

Yaotl is alive! *Figure out what the pictures below have in common to guess who Yaotl really is.*

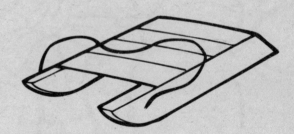

ANSWER: _____.

The Turtles team up with Casey and April for battle.

The Foot Clan protects Winters Tower.

Combat Connect

Who's fighting Karai? *Connect the dots to find out.*

Yaotl prepares to open the portal.

Fake Monster

The portal isn't opening all the way. *Find and circle the creature that doesn't belong.*

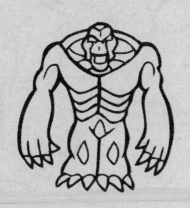

Raphael rescues Leonardo!

Yaotl and the Generals must pass through
the portal to end their curse.

The Generals don't want to go back through the portal.
They want to live forever!

The Foot Ninjas join with April and Casey
to find the final monster.

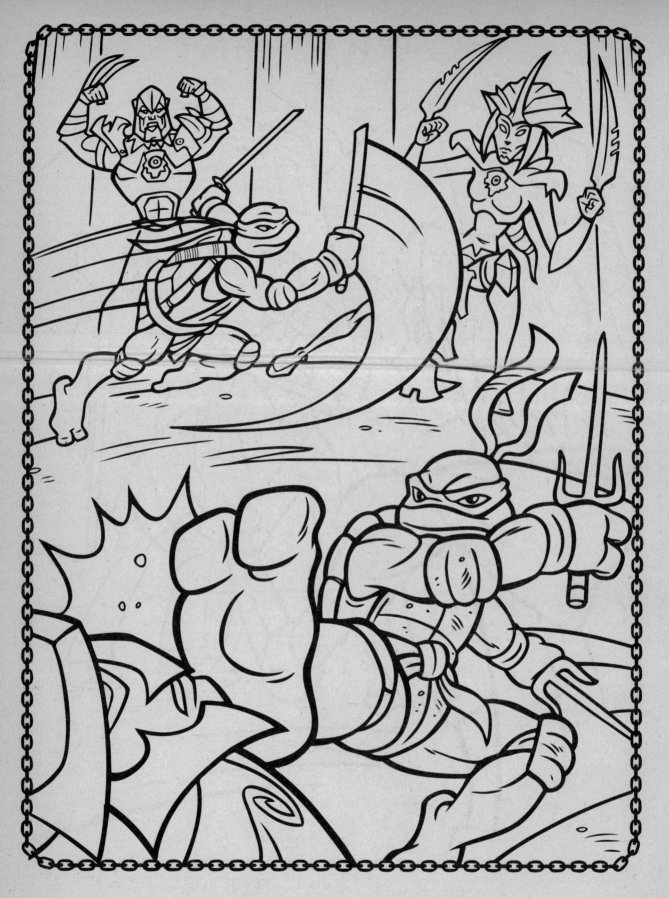

The Turtles take on the Generals!

The Monster Has Arrived

Connect the dots to see the final monster!

The Turtles shove the Generals back into the portal!

They're too strong, and they climb back out.

Yaotl and the final monster push the Generals
back into the portal.

The portal is closed. The battle's over!

Party Time

The Turtles like to celebrate with pizza.
Draw a picture of yourself celebrating with your friends in the box below.

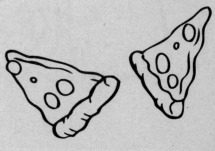

Answers

Page 7
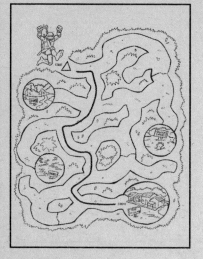

Page 13
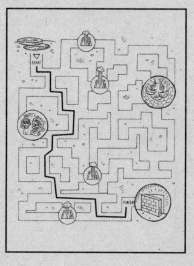

RAPHAEL
1 2 3 4 5 6 7

Page 17

Page 19

MICHELANGELO

Page 22
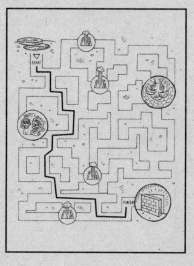

Page 26

Page 28

Page 31

WRITE YOUR ANSWER HERE: HOCKEY

Answers

Page 38

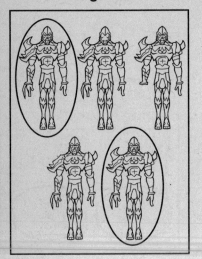

Page 46

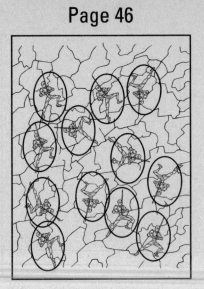

Page 50

Page 53

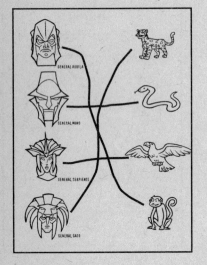

Page 55

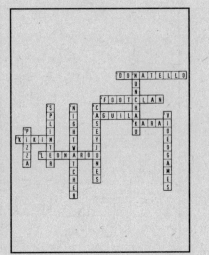

Page 58

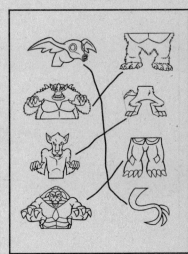

Page 60

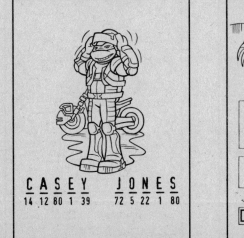

C A S E Y   J O N E S
14 12 80 1 39   72 5 22 1 80

Page 65

Answers

Page 68

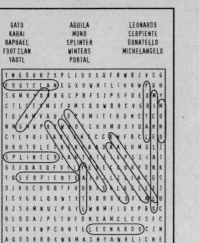

Page 69

N E W   Y O R K   C I T Y !

Page 72

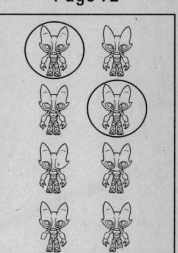

Page 76

ANSWER: WINTERS

Page 79

Page 81

Page 87